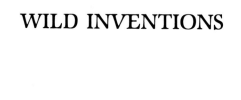

WILD INVENTIONS

WILD INVENTIONS

EDITED BY
Isaac Asimov
Martin Harry Greenberg
Charles Waugh

ILLUSTRATED BY
William Ersland

RAINTREE PUBLISHERS
MILWAUKEE TORONTO MELBOURNE LONDON

Library of Congress Number: 81-8511

1 2 3 4 5 6 7 8 9 0 85 84 83 82 81

Printed in the United States of America.

Library of Congress Cataloging in Publication Data

Main entry under title:

Wild inventions.

  (Science-fiction readers)
  Contents: Introduction / Isaac Asimov — The postponed cure / Stan Nodvik — Man of distinction / Michael Shaara — [etc.]
    1. Science fiction, American. 2. Children's stories, American. [1. Inventions — Fiction. 2. Science fiction. 3. Short stories] I. Asimov, Isaac, 1920-   . II. Greenberg, Martin Harry. III. Waugh, Charles. IV. Ersland, William, 1948-   ill. PZ5.W635   [Fic]   81-8511 ISBN 0-8172-1728-2   AACR2

"The Postponed Cure" © 1974 by Mankind Publishing Company. Reprinted by permission of the Scott Meredith Literary Agency, Inc., 845 Third Ave., New York, NY 10022, on behalf of Mr. Nodvik. Every effort has been made to locate the author.
"Man of Distinction" © 1956 by Galaxy Publishing Corporation. Reprinted by permission of the author and the author's agents, Scott Meredith Literary Agency., Inc., 845 Third Ave., New York, NY 10022.
"Speed of the Cheetah, Roar of the Lion" © 1973 by Mercury Press, Inc. From *The Magazine of Fantasy and Science Fiction*. Reprinted by permission of the author.
"Wapshot's Demon" © 1956 by Columbia Publications, Inc. Reprinted by permission of the author.

Contents

Introduction

ISAAC ASIMOV

One of the things that makes human beings different from all other animals is that human beings not only use tools but invent *new* tools.

An animal might use a rock or pebble to smash shellfish, but only human beings grind a rock to a sharp edge and tie it to a stick to make an axe.

In fact, the only reason human beings control the world the way they do and have no fear of other animals is that they have weapons they have invented. Imagine trying to face elephants, lions or bears without spears, knives, nets or guns — but with just our bare hands.

We would be helpless. We could only run away.

We don't know who invented the earliest devices. We don't know what genius invented the wheel, or the bow and arrow, because in those days no one kept records of that sort of thing. We don't even know who invented some of the great discoveries of the Middle Ages, such as the magnetic compass or the horseshoe.

About the first great inventor we know by name is Tsai Lun, an official at the Chinese Emperor's court about 100 A.D. He worked out a way of making paper from rags.

Then, in 1454, a German inventor, Johann Gutenberg, invented printing. Look about you! Look at everything that is made of paper and that has printing on it. What would life be like if there were no paper and no printing. For that matter, what would life be like if there were no wheels.

After 1454, we know the names of most inventors.

In the last two hundred years, inventing has proceeded at high speed. Many inventions have been made — steamships, locomotives, electric lights, phonographs, telegraphs, telephones, radios, motion pictures, television, automobiles, airplanes, atom bombs, rocket ships. Those are just a few of the great inventions of the period and every one of them has changed the lives of people.

Such inventions seem very ordinary to us now that we are used to them, but they would have seemed wild indeed to people who had lived in earlier times and had never even imagined such things.

Suppose you tried to tell someone from the time of George Washington about pictures that moved and talked and told a story; or automobiles that could move without any horses to pull them and could travel much faster and farther than any horse could manage; or large heavy machines that could be filled with over a hundred people and could then be made to fly through the air, higher and faster than any bird.

He would never believe you. He would consider you crazy.

Not all the results of such inventions might be good. Automobiles are so useful that we can't imagine a world without them — but they kill 50,000 Americans a year and poison the air with their fumes.

Well, then, what kind of inventions will the future hold for us? How wild will they seem to us if we could look into the future and see them? What inconveniences or outright dangers will they bring to us?

This is something that should concern science fiction writers as they try to imagine what the future will be like, as you will see in this book. After all, it could be very important to see in advance what the difficulties and dangers might be in an invention that would look exciting and useful to begin with. We might try to take action to prevent those dangers from the start.

The Postponed Cure

STAN NODVIK

Barnabas and Winona waited anxiously for the doctor to give his diagnosis after a week of what seemed endless tests. The doctor leaned back in his chair and stared unflinchingly at Barnabas and said: "I'd like to level with you, Barney, and tell you the truth. Some medical men believe in keeping something like this from the patient but — "

Winona reached over and clasped his hand for support as Barnabas interrupted. "Give it to me straight, Doc."

"You have six months to live."

Winona gasped and flung her arms about Barnabas's neck. Clinging to him she whimpered softly as the doctor continued to speak.

"You have a rare disease, Barney. One that we know very little about. A disease for which there is no cure — " The doctor paused and, glancing down at his laced fingers, added in a suggestive tone: " — unless . . ."

"Unless what?" Barnabas asked quickly, his voice grabbing at the hint of a remedy like a drowning man trying for a floating life preserver.

"Unless you take what I'd like to call, the postponed cure."

"The what?"

"The postponed cure. It's not actually a cure. It's the chance for a cure. The chance to live to a ripe old age. Listen, Barney. You're a young man." The doctor looked down at the records on his desk. "Twenty-three years old. It is a pity that a man should die so young. But there is an alternative."

Winona cried out in anguish. "What alternative?"

"It's something new. A new method. It's like this: Your body will be given certain drugs that will preserve it until modern medical science finds a cure for your disease."

"Preserve? I don't understand," Barnabas said, puzzled.

"Just what I said. Preserve. You will remain in your present state. There will be no change in your body. You will be technically dead, yet not dead. Let me say instead, you will be asleep, in a deep sleep. You will be brought back to life when a cure is found. Maybe a year or two from now."

Both smiled, welcoming the thought of Barnabas's salvation.

"I'll wait for you, Barney," Winona cried joyfully.

The doctor dispelled their smiles by adding: "Or maybe years from now."

The faces full of joy collapsed like putty. Winona made an O with her lips.

"But will they be able to bring me back to life when . . . whenever they find a cure?"

"Oh yes. Certainly. They've researched it completely and tested it. It's merely a matter of drugs. They give you one drug and you're like petrified wood. Then later when the time comes they give you another drug and you're alive and well."

"Reborn," Winona said in awe.

"Yes, I guess you could say that. There is only one drawback. It costs a great deal of money. This is something completely new, you understand. And for the present time quite costly."

Winona laughed. "Money is of no object. My family are important people. My father left us plenty when he died."

"Well then," the doctor said, standing to signify the conclusion of the interview, "in that case it's a matter of choice. You, Barney, must decide whether you want to live another six months or else take the chance for the postponed cure and for greater longevity. And you, Winona, must decide whether you will wait for Barney. It may be a long wait. Very long."

Winona looked into Barnabas's eyes and smiled. "We have decided. I will wait."

Barnabas opened his lips to speak, but Winona silenced them with the tips of her fingers. "I will wait!" she said.

The curator, seated on his stool amidst the preserved bodies, read the article in the newspaper and marvelled at the wonders of science. Finally they had the cure for . . . for . . . whatever-it-was. He could not pronounce the name of the rare disease even though he slowly mouthed the syllables several times. He shook his head in puzzlement and gave it up.

Then he read the article one more time before he heard the noon-hour chime of the bells outside. He folded the newspaper and tucked it under his arm and headed for Gino's for lunch, leaving the Egyptian mummy room of the Philadelphia University Museum in a hurry.

Man of Distinction

MICHAEL SHAARA

The remarkable distinction of Thatcher Blitt did not come to the attention of a bemused world until late in the year 2180. Although Thatcher Blitt was, by the standards of his time, an extremely successful man financially, this was not considered real distinction. Unfortunately for Blitt, it never has been.

The history books do not record the names of the most successful merchants of the past unless they happened by chance to have been connected with famous men of the time. Thus Croesus is remembered largely for his contributions to famous Romans and successful armies. And Haym Solomon, a similarly wealthy man, would have been long forgotten had he not also been a financial mainstay of the American Revolution and consorted with famous, if impoverished, statesmen.

So if Thatcher Blitt was distinct among men, the distinction was not immediately apparent. He was a small, gaunt, fragile man who had the kind of face and bearing that are perfect for movie crowd scenes. Absolutely forgettable. Yet Thatcher Blitt was one of the foremost businessmen of his time. For he was president and founder of that noble institution, Genealogy, Inc.

Thatcher Blitt was not yet twenty-five when he made the discovery which was to make him among the richest men of his time. His discovery was, like all great ones, obvious yet profound. He observed that every person had a father.

Carrying on with this thought, it followed inevitably that every father had a father, and so on. In fact, thought Blitt, when you considered the matter rightly, everyone alive was the direct descendant of untold numbers of fathers, down through the ages, all descending, one after another, father to son. And so backward, unquestionably, into the unrecognizable and perhaps simian fathers of the past.

This thought, on the face of it not particularly startling, hit young Blitt like a blow. He saw that since each man had a father, and so on and so on, it ought to be possible to construct the genealogy of every person now alive. In short, it should be possible to trace your family back, father by father, to the beginning of time.

And of course it was. For that was the era of the time scanner. And with a time scanner, it would be possible to document your family tree with perfect accuracy. You could find out exactly from whom you had sprung.

And so Thatcher Blitt made his fortune. He saw clearly at the beginning what most of us see only now, and he patented it. He was aware not only of the deep-rooted sense of snobbishness that exists in many people, but also of the simple yet profound force of curiosity. Who exactly, one says to oneself, was my forty-times-great-great-grandfather? A Roman Legionary? A Viking? A pyramid builder? One of Xenophon's Ten Thousand? Or was he, perhaps (for it is always possible), Alexander the Great?

Thatcher Blitt had a product to sell. And sell he did, for other reasons that he alone had noted at the beginning. The races of mankind have twisted and turned with incredible complexity over the years; the numbers of people have been enormous.

With thirty thousand years in which to work, it was impossible that there was not, somewhere along the line, a famous ancestor for everybody. A minor king would often suffice, or even a general in some forgotten army. And if these direct ancestors were not

enough, it was fairly simple to establish close blood kinship with famous men. The bloodlines of man, you see, begin with a very few people. In all of ancient Greece, in the time of Pericles, there were only a few thousand families.

Seeing all this, Thatcher Blitt became a busy man. It was necessary not only to patent his idea, but to produce the enormous capital needed to found a large organization. The cost of the time scanner was at first prohibitive, but gradually the obstacle was overcome, only for Thatcher to find that the government for many years prevented him from using it. Yet Blitt was indomitable. And eventually, after years of heart-rending waiting, Genealogy, Inc., began operations.

It was a tremendous success. Within months, the very name of the company and its taut slogan, "An Ancestor for Everybody," became household words. There was but one immediate draw-back. It soon became apparent that, without going back very far into the past, it was sometimes impossible to tell who was really the next father in line. The mothers were certain, but the fathers were something else again. This was a ponderable point.

But Blitt refused to be discouraged. He set various electronic engineers to work on the impasse and a solution was found. An ingenious device which tested blood electronically through the scanner — based on the different sine waves of the blood groups — saved the day. That invention was the last push Genealogy, Inc., was ever to need. It rolled on to become one of the richest and, for a long while, most exclusive corporations in the world.

Yet it was still many years before Thatcher Blitt himself had time to rest. There were patent infringements to be fought, new developments in the labs to be watched, new ways to be found to make the long and arduous task of father-tracing easier and more economical. Hence he was well past sixty when he at last had time to begin considering himself.

He had become by this time a moderately offensive man. Surrounded as he had been all these years by pomp and luxury, by impressive names and extraordinary family trees, he had succumbed at last. He became unbearably name-conscious.

He began by regrouping his friends according to their ancestries. His infrequent parties were characterized by his almost parliamentarian system of seating. No doubt, all this had been in Thatcher Blitt to begin with — it may well be, in perhaps varying quantities, in all of us — but it grew with him, prospered with him. Yet in all those years he never once inspected his own forebears.

You may well ask, was he afraid? One answers, one does not know. But at any rate, the fact remains that Thatcher Blitt, at the age of sixty-seven, was one of the few rich men in the world who did not know who exactly their ancestors had been.

And so, at last, we come to the day when Thatcher Blitt was sitting alone in his office, one languid hand draped vacantly over his brow, listening with deep satisfaction to the hum and click of the enormous operations which were going on in the building around him.

What moved him that day remains uncertain. Perhaps it was that, from where he was sitting, he could see row upon row of action pictures of famous men which had been taken from his time scanners. Or perhaps it was simply that this profound question had been gnawing at him all these years, deeper and deeper, and on this day broke out into the light.

But whatever the reason, at 11:02 that morning, he leaped vitally from his chair. He summoned Cathcart, his chief assistant, and gave him the immortal command.

"Cathcart!" he grated, stung to the core of his being. "Who am I?"

Cathcart rushed off to find out.

There followed some of the most taut and fateful days in the brilliant history of Genealogy, Inc. Father-tracing is, of course, a painstaking business. But it was not long before word had begun to filter out to interested people.

The first interesting discovery made was a man called Blott, in eighteenth-century England. (No explanation was ever given for the name's alteration from Blott to Blitt. Certain snide individuals took this to mean that the name had been changed as a means to avoid prosecution, or some such, and immediately began making light remarks about the Blotts on old Blitt's escutcheon.) This Blott

had the distinction of having been a wine seller of considerable funds.

This reputedly did not sit well with Thatcher Blitt. Merchants, he snapped, however successful, are not worthy of note. He wanted empire builders. He wanted, at the very least, a name he had heard about. A name that appeared in the histories.

His workers furiously scanned back into the past.

Months went by before the next name appeared. In ninth-century England, there was a wandering minstrel named John (last name unprintable) who achieved considerable notoriety as a ballad singer, before dying an unnatural death in the boudoir of a lady of high fashion. Although the details of this man's life were of extreme interest, they did not impress the old man. He was, on the contrary, rather shaken. A minstrel. And a rogue to boot.

There were shake-ups in Genealogy, Inc. Cathcart was replaced by a man named Jukes, a highly competent man despite his interesting family name. Jukes forged ahead full steam past the birth of Christ (no relation). But he was well into ancient Egypt before the search began to take on the nature of a crisis.

Up until then, there was simply nobody. Or to be more precise, nobody but nobodies. It was incredible, all the laws of chance were against it, but there was, actually, not a single ancestor of note. And no way of faking one, for Thatcher Blitt couldn't be fooled by his own methods. What there was was simply an un-ending line of peasants, serfs, an occasional foot soldier or leather worker. Past John, the ballad singer, there was no one at all worth reporting to the old man.

This situation would not continue, of course. There were so few families for men to spring from. The entire Gallic nation, for example, a great section of present-day France, sprang from the family of one lone man in the North of France in the days before Christ. Every native Frenchman, therefore, was at least the son of a king. It was impossible for Thatcher Blitt to be less.

So the hunt went on from day to day, past ancient Greece, past Jarmo, past the wheel and metals and farming and on even past all civilization, outward and backward into the cold primordial wastes of northern Germany.

And still there was nothing. Though Jukes lived in daily fear of losing his job, there was nothing to do but press on. In Germany he reduced Blitt's ancestor to a slovenly little man who was one of only three men in the entire tribe, or family, one of three in an area which now contains millions. But Blitt's ancestor, true to form, was simply a member of the tribe. As was his father before him.

Yet onward it went. Westward back into the French caves, southward into Spain and across the unrecognizable Mediterranean into a verdant North Africa, backward in time past even the Cro-Magnons, and yet ever backward, 30,000 years, 35,000, with old Blitt reduced now practically to gibbering and still never an exceptional forebear.

There came a time when Jukes had at last, inevitably, to face the old man. He had scanned back as far as he could. The latest ancestor he had unearthed for Blitt was a hairy creature who did not walk erect. And yet, even here, Blitt refused to concede.

"It may be," he howled, "it must be that my ancestor was the first man to walk erect or light a fire — to do something."

It was not until Jukes pointed out that all those things had been already examined and found hopeless that Blitt finally gave in. Blitt was a relative, of course, of the first man to stand erect, the man with the first human brain. But so was everybody else on the face of the Earth. There was truly nowhere else to explore. What would be found now would be only the common history of mankind.

Blitt retired to his chambers and refused to be seen.

The story went the rounds, as such stories will. And it was then at last, after 40,000 years of insignificance, that the name of Blitt found everlasting distinction. The story was picked up, fully documented, by psychologists and geneticists of the time, and inserted into textbooks as a profound commentary on the forces of heredity. The name of Thatcher Blitt in particular has become famous, has persisted until this day. For he is the only man yet discovered, or ever likely to be discovered, with this particular distinction.

In 40,000 years of scanner-recorded history, the bloodline of Blitt (or Blott) never once produced an exceptional man.

That record is unsurpassed.

Speed of the Cheetah, Roar of the Lion

HARRY HARRISON

"Here he comes, Dad," Billy shouted, waving the field glasses. "He just turned the corner from Lilac."

Henry Brogan grunted a bit as he squeezed behind the wheel of his twenty-two-foot-long, eight-foot-wide, three hundred and sixty-horsepower, four-door, power-everything and air-conditioning, definitely not compact, luxury car. There was plenty of room between the large steering wheel and the back of the leather-covered seat, but there was plenty of Henry as well, particularly around the middle. He grunted again as he leaned over to turn the ignition switch. The thunderous roar of unleashed horsepower filled the garage, and he smiled with pleasure.

Billy squatted behind the hedge, peering through it, and when he called out again, his voice squeaked with excitement.

"A block away and slowing down!"

"Here we go!" his father called out gaily, pressing down on the accelerator. The roar of the exhaust was like thunder, and the open garage doors vibrated with the sound while every empty can bounced upon the shelves. Out of the garage the great machine charged, down the drive and into the street with the grace and majesty of an unleashed 747. Roaring with the voice of freedom, it surged majestically past the one-cylinder, plastic and plywood, one hundred and thirty-two miles to the gallon, single-seater Austerity Beetle that Simon Pismire was driving. Simon was just turning into his own driveway when the behemoth of the highways hurtled by and set his tiny conveyance rocking in the slipstream. Simon, face red with fury, popped up through the open top like a gopher from his hole and shook his fist after the car with impotent rage, his words lost in the roar of the eight gigantic cylinders. Henry Brogan admired this in his mirror, and laughed with glee.

It was indeed a majestic sight, a whale among the shoals of minnows. The tiny vehicles that cluttered the street parted before him, their drivers watching his passage with bulging eyes. The pedestrians and bicyclists, on the newly poured sidewalks and bicycle paths, were no less attentive or impressed. The passage of a king in his chariot, or an All-American on the shoulders of his teammates, would have aroused no less interest. Henry was indeed King of the Road and he gloated with pleasure.

Yet he did not go far; that would be rubbing their noses in it. His machine waited, rumbling with restrained impatience at the light, then turned into Hollywood Boulevard, where he stopped before the Thrifty drugstore. He left the engine running, muttering happily to itself, when he got out, and pretended not to notice the stares of everyone who passed.

"Never looked better," Doc Kline said. The druggist met him at the door and handed him his four-page copy of the weekly Los Angeles Times. "Sure in fine shape."

"Thanks, Doc. A good car should have good care taken of it." They talked a minute about the usual things: the blackouts on the East Coast, schools closed by the power shortage, the new emergency message from the President, about Lake Erie drying up; then Henry strolled back and threw the paper in onto the seat. He was just opening the door when Simon Pismire came popping slowly up in his Austerity Beetle.

"Get good mileage on that thing, Simon?" Henry asked innocently.

"Listen to me, you old fool! You come charging out in that tank, almost run me down, I'll have the law on you —"

"Now, Simon, I did nothing of the sort. Never came near you. And I looked around careful like because that little thing of yours is hard to see at times."

Simon's face was flushed with rage and he danced little angry steps upon the sidewalk. "Don't talk to me like that! I'll have the law on you with that truck, burning our priceless oil reserves —"

"Watch the temper, Simon. The old ticker can go poof if you let yourself get excited. You're in the coronary belt now, you know. And you also know the law's been around my place often. The price and rationing people, IRS, police, everyone. They did admire my car, and all of them shook hands like gentlemen when they left. The law likes my car, Simon. Isn't that right, Officer?"

O'Reilly, the beat cop, was leaning his bike against the wall, and he waved and hurried on, not wanting to get involved. "Fine by me, Mr. Brogan," he called back over his shoulder as he entered the store.

"There, Simon, you see?" Henry slipped behind the wheel and tapped the gas pedal; the exhaust roared and people stepped quickly back onto the curb. Simon pushed his head in the window and shouted.

"You're just driving this car to bug me, that's all you're doing!" His face was, possibly, redder now and sweat beaded his forehead. Henry smiled and winked broadly before answering.

"Now that's not a nice thing to say. We've been neighbors for years, you know. Remember when I bought a Chevy how the very next week you had a two-door Buick? I got a nice buy on a secondhand four-door Buick, but you had a new Tornado the same day. Just by coincidence, I guess. Like when I built a twenty-foot swimming pool, you, just by chance, I'm sure, had a thirty-foot one dug that was even a foot deeper than mine. These things never bothered me — "

"Ha! Mebbe you *think* they didn't!"

"Well, maybe they did. But they don't bother me any more, Simon, not any more."

He stepped lightly on the accelerator, and the juggernaut of the road surged away and around the corner and was gone. As he drove, Henry could not remember a day when the sun had shone more clearly from a smogless sky, nor when the air had smelled fresher. It was a beautiful day indeed.

Billy was waiting by the garage when he came back, closing and locking the door when the last high, gleaming fender had rolled by. He laughed out loud when his father told him what had happened, and before the story was done, they were both weak with laughter.

"I wish I could have seen his face, Dad, I really do. I tell you what for tomorrow, why don't I turn up the volume on the exhaust a bit. We got almost two hundred watts of output from the amplifier, and that is a twelve-inch speaker down there between the rear wheels. What do you say?"

"Maybe, just a little bit, a little bit more each day maybe. Let's look at the clock." He squinted at the instrument panel, and the smile drained from his face. "Will you look at that! I had eleven minutes of driving time. I didn't know it was that long."

"Eleven minutes . . . that will be about two hours."

"I know — just don't rub it in. But spell me a bit, will you, or I'll be too tired to eat dinner."

Billy took the big crank out of the tool box and opened the cover of the gas cap and fitted the socket end of the crank over the hex stud inside. Henry spat on his hands and seized the two-foot-long handle and began cranking industriously.

"I don't care if it takes two hours to wind up the spring," he panted. "It was worth every single second of it."

Wapshot's Demon

FREDERIK POHL

He kept me waiting on a hard wooden bench for three-quarters of an hour before his secretary came wandering out, glanced casually at me, stopped to chat with the switchboard girl, drifted in my direction again, paused to straighten out the magazines on the waiting-room table, and finally came over to tell me that the Postal Inspector would see me now.

I was in no mood to be polite, but I was very good. I marched in and put my briefcase on his desk and said, "Sir, I must protest this high-handed behavior. I assure you, I have no client whose activities would bring him in conflict in any way with the Post Office Department. I said as much to one of your staff on the phone, after I received your letter ordering me to appear here, but they — "

He stood up, smiling amiably, and shook my hand before I could get it out of the way. "That's all right," he said cheerfully. "That's perfectly all right. We'll straighten it out right away. What did you say your name was?"

I told him my name and started to go on with what I had to say, but he wasn't listening. "Roger Barclay," he repeated, looking at a pile of folders on his desk. "Barclay, Barclay, Barclay. Oh, yes."

He picked up one of the folders and opened it. "The Wapshot business," he said.

The folder seemed to contain mostly large, bright-colored, flimsy-looking magazines entitled Secret, Most Secret, Top Secret and Shush! He opened one of them where a paper clip marked a place and handed it to me. There was a small ad circled in red crayon. "That's it," he said. "Your boy Wapshot."

The ad was of no conceivable interest to me; I barely glanced at it, something about fortune-telling, it looked like, signed by somebody named Cleon Wapshot at an address in one of those little towns in Maine. I handed it back to the Postal Inspector. "I have already informed you," I said, "That I have no client involved in difficulties with the Post Office Department; that is not my sort of practice at all. And I most certainly have no client named Cleon Wapshot."

That took some of the wind out of his sails. He looked at me suspiciously, then took a scrawly piece of paper out of the folder and read it over, then looked at me suspiciously again. He handed over the piece of paper. "What about this, then?" he demanded.

It was a penciled letter, addressed to the Postal Inspector in Eastport, Maine; it said:

Dear Sir:
Please send all further communications to my Attorney, Roger Barclay, Esq., of 404 Fifth Avenue, New York, and oblige,
Yours sincerely,
Cleon Wapshot

Naturally, that was a puzzler to me. But I finally convinced the Postal Inspector that I'd never heard of this Wapshot. You could see he thought there was something funny about the whole thing and wasn't quite sure whether I had anything to do with it or not. But, after all, the Post Office Department is used to cranks and he finally let me go, and even apologized for taking my time, after I had assured him for the tenth time that I had nothing to do with Wapshot.

That shows how wrong you can be. I hurried back to my office and went through the private door down the hall. When I rang for

Phoebe I had already put the affair out of my mind, as the sort of ridiculous time-waster that makes it so difficult to run a law office on schedule. Phoebe was bursting with messages; Frankel had called on the Harry's Hideaway lease, call him back; Mr. Zimmer had called three times, wouldn't leave a message; the process server had been unable to find the defendants in the Herlihy suit; one of the operatives from the Splendid Detective Agency was bringing in a confidential report at 3:30. "And there's a man to see you," she finished up. "He's been here over an hour; his name's, uh, Wapshot, Cleon Wapshot."

He was a plump little man with a crew cut. Not very much like any Down-East lobsterman I ever had imagined, but his voice was authentic of the area. I said, "Sir, you have caused me a great deal of embarrassment. What in heaven's name possessed you to give the Post Office my name?"

He blinked at me mildly. "You're my lawyer."

"Nonsense! My good man, there are some formalities to go through before — "

"Pshaw," he said, "here's your retainer, Mr. Barclay." He pushed a manila envelope toward me across the desk.

I said, "But I haven't taken your case — "

"You will."

"But the retainer — I scarcely know what the figure should be. I don't even know what law you br — what allegations were made."

"Oh, postal fraud, swindling, fortune-telling, that kind of thing," he said. "Nothing to it. How much you figure you ought to have just to get started?"

I sat back and looked him over. Fortune-telling! Postal fraud! But he had a round-faced honesty, you know, the kind of expression jurymen respect and trust. He didn't look rich and he didn't look poor; he had a suit on that was very far from new, but the overcoat was new, brand-new, and not cheap. And besides he had come right out and said what his business was; none of this fake air of "I don't need a lawyer, but if you want to pick up a couple of bucks for saving me the trouble of writing a letter, you're on" that I see coming in to my office thirty times a week.

I said briskly, "Five hundred dollars for a starter, Mr. Wapshot."

He grinned and tapped the envelope. "Count 'er up," he said.

I stared at him, but I did what he said. I dumped the contents of the manila envelope on my desk.

There was a thick packet of U. S. Postal Money Orders — a hundred and forty-one of them, according to a neatly penciled slip attached to them, made out variously to — "Cleon Wapshot," "Clion Wopshatt," "C. Wapshut" and a dozen other alternate forms, each neatly endorsed on the back by my new client, each in the amount of $1.98.

There was a packet, not quite so thick, of checks, all colors and sizes; ninety-six of these, all in the same amount of $1.98.

There was a still thinner packet of one-dollar bills — thirty of them; and finally there were stamps amounting to 74¢. I took a pencil and added them up:

$$\$ \ 279.18$$
$$190.08$$
$$30.00$$
$$.74$$
$$\$ 500.00$$

Wapshot said anxiously, "That's all right, isn't it? I'm sorry about the stamps, but that's the way the orders come in and there's nothing I can do about it — I tried and tried to turn them in, but they won't give me but half the value for them in the post office, and that's not right. That's wasteful. You can use them around here, can't you?"

I said with an effort, "Sit down, Mr. Wapshot. Tell me what this is all about."

Well, he told me. But whether I understood or didn't understand I can't exactly say. Parts of it made sense, and parts of it were obviously crazy.

But what it all came to was that, with five appointments and a heavy day's mail untouched, I found myself in a cab with this Cleon Wapshot, beetling across town to a little fleabag hotel on the West Side. I didn't think the elevator was going to make it, but I have to admit I was wrong. It got us to the fifth floor, and Wapshot led the way down a hall where all the doors seemed to be ajar and the guests peeping impassively out at us, and we went into a room with an unmade bed and a marble-topped bureau and a dripping shower in the pint-sized bath, and a luggage rack and — on the luggage rack, a washing machine.

Or anyway, it looked like a washing machine.

Wapshot put his hand on it with simple pride.

"My Semantic Polarizer," he explained.

I followed him into the room, holding my breath. There was a fine, greasy film of grit on the gadget — Wapshot had not been clever enough to close the window to the airshaft, which appeared to double as a garbage chute for the guests on the upper stories. Under the grit — as I say, a washing machine. One of the small light-housekeeping kinds: a drawn aluminum pail, a head with some sort of electric business inside. And a couple of things that didn't seem connected with washing clothes — two traps, one on either side of the pail. The traps were covered with wire mesh, and both of them were filled with white cards.

"Here," said Wapshot, and picked one of the cards out of the nearest trap. It was a tiny snapshot, like the V-mail letters, photographically diminished, soldiers overseas used to send. I read it without difficulty:

> Dear Mr. Wapshot,
>   My Husband was always a good Husband to me, not counting the Drink, but when his Cousin moved in upstairs he cooled off to me. He is always buying her Candy and Flowers because he promised her Mother he would take care of her after the Mother, who was my Husband's Aunt, died. Her Television is always getting broken and he has to go up to fix it, sometimes until four o'clock in the Morning. Also, he never told me he had an Aunt until she moved in. I enclose $1 Dollar and .98 Cents as it says in your ad. in SHUT UP!, please tell me, is she really his Cousin?

I looked up from the letter. Wapshot took it from me, glanced at it, shrugged. "I get a lot of that kind," he said.

"Mr. Wapshot, are you confessing that you are telling fortunes by mail?"

"No!" He looked upset. "Didn't I make you understand? It hasn't got anything to do with fortunes. Questions that have a yes or no answer, that's all — if I can give them a definite yes or a definite no, I do it and keep the dollar ninety-eight. If I can't I give back the money."

I stared at him, trying to tell if he was joking. He didn't look as though he was joking. In the airshaft something went whiz-pop; a fine spray of grit blew in off the window sill.

Wapshot shook his head reproachfully. "Throwing their trash down again. Mr. Barclay, I've told the desk clerk a dozen times — "

"Forget the desk clerk! What's the difference between what you said and fortune-telling?"

He took a deep breath. "I swear, Mr. Barclay," he said sadly, "I don't think you listen. I went all through this in your office."

"Do it again."

He shrugged. "Well," he said, "you start with Clerk Maxwell. He was a man who discovered a lot of things, and one of the things he discovered he never knew about."

I yelled, "Now, how could he — "

"Just listen, Mr. Barclay. It was something that they call 'Maxwell's Demon.' You know what hot air is?"

I said, meaning it to hurt, "I'm learning."

"No, no, not that kind of hot air. I mean just plain hot air, like you might get out of a radiator. It's hot because the molecules in it are moving fast. Understand? Heat is fast molecules, cold is slow molecules. That's the only difference." He was getting warmed up. "Now, ordinary air," he went on, "is a mixture of molecules at different speeds. Some move fast, some move slow; it's the average that gives you your temperature. What Clerk Maxwell said, and he said it kind of as a joke, you know — except a genius never really jokes, and never really makes a mistake; even the things he doesn't really mean sometimes turn out to be true — Anyway, what Clerk Maxwell said was, 'Wouldn't it be nice if we could train a little demon to stand in the window of a house. He could direct the fast-moving molecules inside, giving us heat, and direct the slow-moving ones into, say, the kitchen refrigerator — giving us cold.' You follow me so far?"

I laughed. "Ha-ha. But I'm not a fool, Mr. Wapshot, and I have had a certain amount of education. I am aware that there is a law of entropy that — "

"Ha-ha," he interrupted. "Hold on for a minute, Mr. Barclay. I heard all about the law of entropy, which says that high and low temperatures tend to merge and average out, instead of separating. I heard about it, you heard about it, and even Maxwell heard about it. But there was a German fellow name of Hilsch, and he didn't hear about it. Because what he did, Mr. Barclay, was to invent something called the 'Hilsch Tube,' and all the Hilsch tube is is Maxwell's demon come to life. Honest. It really works. You blow into it — it's a kind of little pipe with a joint sticking out of it, the simplest-looking little thing you ever saw — and hot air comes out of one end, cold air comes out of the other. Don't take my word for it," he said hurriedly, holding up his hand. "Don't argue with me. After World War II, they brought back a couple of those things from Germany, and they're all over the country now. They work."

I said patiently, "Mr. Wapshot, what has this got to do with fortune-telling?"

He scowled. "It isn't fortune — Well, never mind that. So we take my Semantic Polarizer. I put into it a large sample of particles — what we call a 'universe.' These particles are microfilmed copies of letters people have sent me, along with their checks for a dollar ninety-eight, just like I told them to do in my ads. I run the Polarizer for a while, until the particles in the 'universe' are thoroughly randomed, and then I start tapping off the questions. The ones that come out at this end, the answer is 'yes.' The ones that come out at the other, 'no.' I have to admit," he confessed, a little embarrassed, "that I can only pull about sixty per cent out before the results begin getting unreliable — the ones that come off slowly are evidently less charged than the ones that come off right away, and so there's a chance of error. But the ones that come off early, Mr. Barclay, they're for sure. After all," he de-

manded, "what else can they be but definite? Don't forget, the particles are exactly alike in every respect — shape, color, weight, size, texture, appearance, feel, everything — every respect but one. The only difference is, for some the answer is 'yes,' for some the answer is 'no.' "

I stood looking at him silently.

A bottle whizzed and splintered in the airshaft; we both ducked.

I said, "It works?"

"It works," he said solemnly.

"You've tried it out?"

He grinned — almost for the first time. "You took my case, didn't you? That was a yes. Your price was five hundred? That was a yes. It works, Mr. Barclay. As I see it, that ends the discussion."

And so it did, of course — permanently.

The Semantic Polarizer was remarkably easy to run. I played with it for a while, and then I sent the white-haired bellboy down for the Sunday papers. He looked at me as if I was some kind of an idiot. "Excuse me," he said, scratching his head, "but isn't today Wednes — "

"I want the Sunday papers," I told him. "Here." Well, the five-dollar bill got the papers for me, but obviously he still thought I was crazy. He said:

"Excuse me, but did the gemmun in this room go out?"

"You mean Mr. Wapshot?" I asked him. "Yes. That's right. He went out. And now, if you will kindly do the same . . ."

I locked the door behind him. Oh, Wapshot had gone out, all right. I pulled the papers apart — they were a stack nearly a foot high — and crumpled them section by section and when I dumped them down the airshaft piece by piece, stare how I might, lean as far out as I would, I could see nothing at the bottom of the shaft but paper.

So much for Cleon Wapshot, gone early to join the immortals.

I checked the room over carefully. There was one small blood spot on the floor, but in that room it hardly mattered. I pulled the leg of the chair over to cover it, put the Semantic Analyzer in its crate, turned off the light and rang for the elevator. The blasted thing weighed a ton, but I managed it.

The elevator starter at my office gave me a lot of trouble, but I finally got the thing into a freight elevator and — for another five bucks to the porter — in the private door to my office. Phoebe heard me moving around and came trotting in with a face like cataclysm. "Mr. Barclay," she cried, "they're here! They've been waiting ever since you left with Mr. Wapshot."

"God rest him," I said. "Who are you talking about?"

"Why, the men from the Bar Association," she explained. It had completely slipped my mind.

I patted her hand. "There," I said. "Show them in, my dear."

The two men from the Bar Association came in like corpse robbers. "Mr. Barclay," the fat one said, "speaking for the Committee, we cannot accept your explanation that $11,577.16 of the Hoskins Estates was expended for 'miscellany.' Lacking a more detailed accounting, we have no choice but to — "

"I understand perfectly," I told him, bowing. "You wish me to pay back — to make up the deficit out of my own pocket."

He scowled at me. "Why — yes, that for a starter," he said sternly. "But there is also the matter of the Annie Sprayragen Trust Fund, where the item of $9,754.08 for 'general expense' has been challenged by — "

"That too," I said. "Gentlemen, I shall pauperize myself to make good these sums. My whole fortune will go to it, if necessary."

"Fortune!" squawked the short, thin one. "That's the trouble, Barclay! We've talked to your bank, and they say you haven't two dimes to rub together!"

"Disbarment!" snarled the fat one. "That's why we're here, Barclay!"

It was time to make an end. I gave up the pretense of politeness. "Gentlemen," I said crisply, "I think not."

They stared. "Barclay," snapped the fat one, "bluff will get you — "

"There's no bluff." I walked over to my desk, patting the crate of the Semantic Polarizer on the way. I pretended to consult my calendar. "Be good enough to return on Monday next," I told them. "I shall have certified checks for the full amounts ready at that time."

The short, thin one said uncertainly, "Why should we let you stall?"

"What else can you do? The money's gone, gentlemen. If you want it back, be here on Monday. And now, good-day."

Phoebe appeared to show them out.

And I got down to work.

Busy, busy, busy.

Phoebe was busier than I, at that — after the first day. I spent the rest of that day printing out yes-or-no questions on little squares of paper, microfilming them and bouncing them through the hopper of the Semantic Polarizer. While the drum of the machine spun and bounced, I stood and gloated.

Wapshot's Demon! And all he could think to use it for was a simple mail-order business, drudgery instead of wealth beyond dreaming. With a brain that could create the Semantic Polarizer, he was unable to see beyond the cash value of a fortune-telling service. Well, it was an easy way to pay his bills, and obviously he wasn't much interested in wealth.

But I, however, was.

And that was why I ran poor Phoebe ragged. To the bookmakers; to the bank; to the stockbrokers; to the track; to the numbers runners; back to the office. I loaned her my pigskin case, and when that wasn't big enough — the numbers bank, for instance, paid off in fives and tens — she took a hundred dollars out of the bottom file drawer and bought a suitcase. Because it was, after all, simple enough to get rich in a hurry. Take a race at Aqueduct; there are eight horses entered, maybe; write a slip for each one: Will ---------- win the first at Aqueduct today? Repeat for the second race, the third race, all the races to the end of the day; run them through the Polarizer, pick out the cards that come through the "yes" hopper —

And place your bets.

Numbers? You need thirty slips. Will the first digit of the winning number be 1, 2, 3, 4-etc. Ten slips for the first digit, ten for the second, ten for the third; pick out the three that come out "yes," put them together, and —

A bet on the numbers pays odds of 600 to 1.

It took me thirty-six hours to work out the winners of the first three weeks' races, fights, ball games and tennis matches; the stock quotations of a hundred selected issues, and the numbers that would come up on the policy wheel. And, I say this, they were the happiest thirty-six hours of my life.

Of all my life.

It was a perfectly marvelous time, and too bad that it couldn't go on. I had everything ready: My suitcase of currency, my lists of the bets to place in the immediate future, my felt-lined wardrobe trunk for transporting the Polarizer, my anonymous letter to the manager of the late Cleon Wapshot's hotel, directing his attention to the airshaft; even my insulting note to the Committee on Disbarments of the Bar Association. My passport was in order, my reservation by Air France to New Guinea was confirmed, and I was only waiting for Phoebe to come back with the tickets. I had time to kill.

And Curiosity is a famed killer. Of cats. Of time. And of other things.

When Phoebe came back she pounded on the door for nearly an hour, knowing I was in there, knowing I would miss my plane, begging me to come out, to answer, to speak to her. But what was the use? I took my list of bets and tore it in shreds. I took the Polarizer and smashed it to jangling bits. And then I waited.

Good-bye, Wall Street! Good-bye, Kentucky Derby. Good-bye, a million dollars a month. I suppose they'll find Wapshot's body sooner or later, and there isn't a doubt that they'll trace it back to me — the bellboy, the postal inspector, even Phoebe might provide the link. Say, a week to find the body; another week, at the most, to put the finger on me. Two months for the trial, and sentence of execution a month or two after. Call it four months from date until they would put me in the chair.

I wish I hadn't asked the Polarizer one certain question.

I wish I were going still to be alive, four months from date.